2: Adriel

Aim: your sexy baby mama !

I ♥ u !

Lady temper

(713) 724 - 84 18

call
me   24/7
baby

To Marion and Eugene

www.houghtonmifflinbooks.com

The text of this book is set in Berthold Block.
The illustrations are gouache.

Warm thanks to Margaret Raymo for her continuing encouragement
and for her unique vision which I am honored to be a part of.
And to Bob Kosturko for his careful eye and always helpful guidance.

Library of Congress Cataloging-in-Publication Data

Montenegro, Laura Nyman.
A bird about to sing / written and illustrated by Laura Nyman Montenegro.
p. cm.
Summary: Natalie, who likes to write poems, goes to a poetry reading and
discovers that a poem needs to be read out loud at just the right time.
ISBN 0-618-18865-7 (hardcover)
[1. Poetry–Fiction.] I. Title.
PZ7.M7635 Bi 2003
[Fic]–dc21
2002005091

Manufactured in the United States of America
WOZ 10 9 8 7 6 5 4 3 2 1

A BIRD
ABOUT TO SING

Written and illustrated by
Laura Nyman Montenegro

Houghton Mifflin Company
Boston 2003

Hi. I'm Natalie.
I am a poet.

And this is Monica.
She's my poetry teacher.

Here is a poem I wrote.

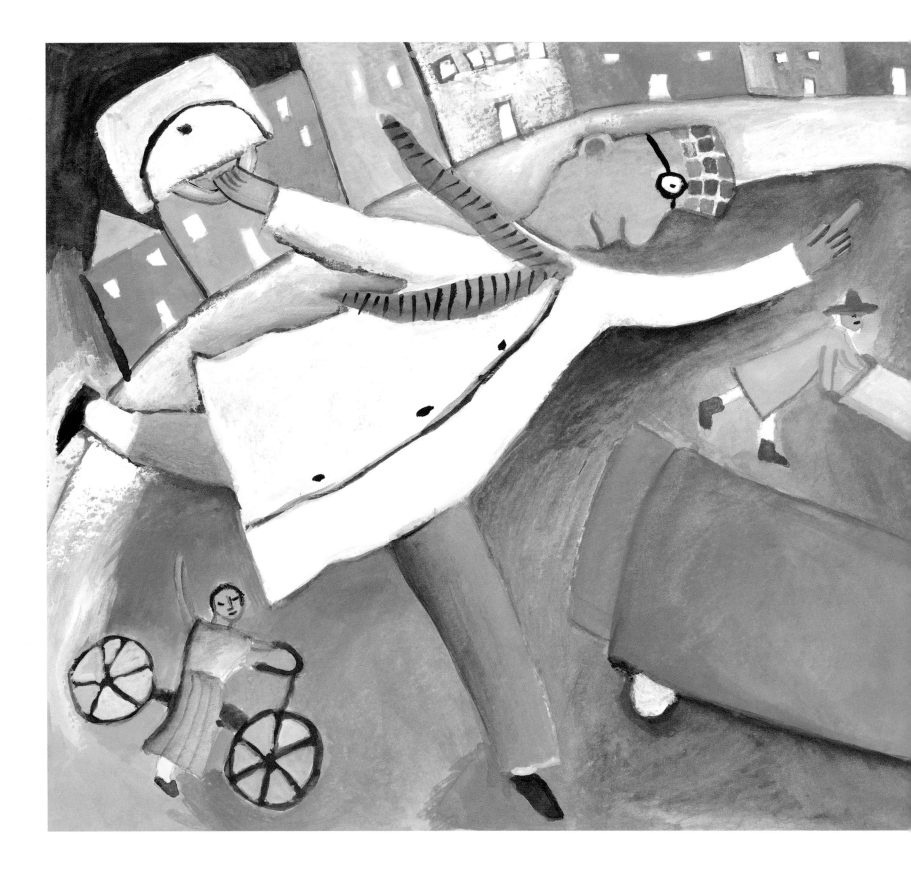

LAST CHANCE, AMBULANCE,

ROMANCE?

You see, I can't help writing poems.
My mother says, "Natalie, you're a natural."
And so does Monica.
But she wants me to read OUT LOUD.

Nope. No way. Never!
When it comes to reading out loud
I'm as silent as a cloud.
Because I'm afraid to read out loud.
But I've decided I'm going to try.

So guess what?
Today Monica is taking me downtown to a poetry reading,
where I will meet all her poet friends.

And she has asked ME to read my poem.

I am wearing my new dress
and my new shoes
and we are riding on the No. 27 bus.
The ride seems short.
We step off the bus and climb
the long staircase.

We knock on the big blue door.

Suddenly, we are in a room full of . . .

POETS!

Monica says hello to her friends.
When everyone is seated, we begin.

Gunther recites his poem
with a booming voice,

and Katerina's voice
makes a little squeak.

Edgar doesn't speak his poems—
he *dances* them.

And Lazlo with his tangled hair
and giant eyebrows
recites a crazy poem
that makes no sense to me.
But everyone laughs and cheers.

Then Monica hushes the crowd
and invites me to read my poem.
I blush and swallow and feel
the eyes of everyone on me.
And suddenly I feel like a bird
who's lost its voice, and like a bird
I wish to fly far, far away
to the top of the tallest tree.
Everyone waits as I stare down at my poem,
and after what seems like hours of silence,
Monica puts her arm around me.
Ethel, with her giant earrings,
yells from the back of the room,
"Give Natalie a cupcake!"
And everyone cheers and begins to talk.

I escaped this time.
No way am I going to stand
up there like a fool again.
I'll read to my cat,
or write a poem on a stick,
or fill my book until it bursts,
but no way will I have all those eyes
on ME.
I tell Monica that I want to go home.
I grab my coat and pull Monica
through the crowd.
Just as I get to the door,
Ethel stops me.
She puts her big face close to mine.
"Don't worry, hon," she says.
"When the time is right,
the bird begins to sing."

The bus is crowded.

Monica says her feet hurt.

We sit quietly on our long ride home.

Then I begin to cry.

"What if I never read out loud?" I say.

"What if I try again and still no words come out?"

Monica takes out her big green handkerchief

so I can blow my nose.

I look out the window. As we wind through the streets of the big city, everything I see suggests a poem:

the black garden dirt with the yellow tulips about to open,

the fire engine going, "E-e-e-e-e-e-,"

and the little girls dancing

as they wait to cross the street.

And then I get this funny feeling.
I feel like a bird
when the sun first breaks.
I feel like a bird about to sing.
"Can I read my poem to you?"
I whisper to Monica.
She smiles.

I stand up and take out a poem.
I read it, softly at first,
then louder and louder.

Can anyone know how I feel?
When horses neigh?
When bumblebees play?
When lightning scratches the sky?

When the moon steps into
her starry boat
on a river of black velvet night?

When hungry dogs chase
thirsty cats
through puddles like
scraps of sky?

When all at once
the tree is full
of berries
that smell like ice?

Yes, can anyone know how I feel?

How I feel right now?

Everyone cheers. "Bravo! Hooray for Natalie."
I turn around and everyone on the bus is clapping.
The bus is full of poets.
There is Gunther and Ethel and Katerina and Lazlo.
You see, poets always ride the bus.

AND I AM A POET, TOO!